The Camel's Back

Scott Fitzgerald

The Camel's Back
First published in the "Saturday Evening Post" in 1920.
First published in book form in "Tales of the Jazz Age" in 1922.
Copyright © 1920 Scott Fitzgerald

This minimally edited edition first published 2018
Copyright © 2018 Erin Pater
Copyright & TransMedia IP are both managed by
Bill4 Ltd, Manchester England

Cover Art: Pablo Picasso "Camel" 1907

ISBN-10: 1943341052
ISBN-13: 978-1943341054

Collector's Item

This wonderful little book is printed using state-of-the-art print-on-demand technology and serves as a time capsule chronicling the evolution of this technology.

To ensure that this wonderful little book maintains its status as a time capsule, we have decided to print only 1,000 copies of this edition, so each surviving copy would appreciate in value as time passes by.

The number of copies printed is audited by Bill4 Ltd of Manchester England, the intellectual property rights management company of this edition. That is why this wonderful little book makes for a perfect gift item to a real loved one.

Contents

This is a Picasso

I was in Malaga Spain, warmly chatting in bed with a flapper girlfriend, our faces close together, our noses almost touching.

"This is a Picasso!" exclaimed my girlfriend.

"What?" came my quick answer.

"Look, look. This is a Picasso!" She said again.

I gazed attentively at her face and there it was, a Picasso. One of her eyes were higher than the other, eyebrow and all, and her nose was hazily split vertically in the middle. Being so close to her face created the illusion that her face was divided in the middle with one side appearing in a higher plane than the other, a cubist painting.

An eureka moment dawned on both of us and we enjoyed the enlightened impression that we kind of understood how Picasso stumbled on Cubism.

We hurriedly got out of bed and rushed to the Picasso museum for the fifth time during our visit, but this time we saw it in a completely different light.

When I first read Scott Fitzgerald's "*The Camel's Back*" I experienced the same feeling. This is a Picasso, a wordsmith's Picasso, painted in colorful words instead of being painted with oil on canvas.

The cubist part, in my opinion, has to do with how Fitzgerald painted his characters. Perry Parkhurst, the man, is painted in full color with rich textures and many undertones:

"I want you to meet Mr. Perry Parkhurst, twenty-eight, lawyer, native of Toledo. Perry has nice teeth, a Harvard diploma, parts his hair in the middle. You have met him before— in Cleveland, Portland, St. Paul, Indianapolis, Kansas City, and so forth. Baker Brothers, New York, pause on their semi-annual trip through the West to clothe him; Montmorency & Co. dispatch a young man post-haste every three months to see that he has the correct number of little punctures on his shoes. He has a domestic roadster now, will have a French roadster if he lives long enough, and doubtless a Chinese tank if it comes into fashion. He looks like the advertisement of the young man rubbing his sunset-colored chest with liniment and goes East every other year to his class reunion."

While Betty Medill, the woman, is rendered in a single shade of light gray:

"I want you to meet his Love. Her name is Betty Medill, and she would take well in the movies. Her father gives her three hundred a month to dress on, and she has tawny eyes and hair and feather fans of five colors."

Of course, he was a man!

Now, I have a suggestion for all aspiring young women writers out there, go ahead, give it a try. Take a stab at writing a mirror image short of *"The Camel's Back"* with Betty Medill in the lead. Take your mental brushes out and go for another Picasso, but this time do try to render more color and more texture to Betty's inner life.

"*I suppose that of all the stories I have ever written this one cost me the least travail and perhaps gave me the most amusement. As to the labor involved, it was written during one day in the city of New Orleans, with the express purpose of buying a platinum and diamond wrist watch which cost six hundred dollars. I began it at seven in the morning and finished it at two o'clock the same night.*"

F. Scott Fitzgerald

Chapter 1

The glazed eye of the tired reader resting for a second on the above title will presume it to be merely metaphorical. Stories about the cup and the lip and the bad penny and the new broom rarely have anything to do with cups or lips or pennies or brooms. This story is the exception. It has to do with a material, visible and large-as-life camel's back.

Starting from the neck we shall work toward the tail. I want you to meet Mr. Perry Parkhurst, twenty-eight, lawyer, native of Toledo. Perry has nice teeth, a Harvard diploma, parts his hair in the middle. You have met him before— in Cleveland, Portland, St. Paul, Indianapolis, Kansas City, and so forth.

Baker Brothers, New York, pause on their semi-annual trip through the West to clothe him; Montmorency & Co. dispatch a young man post-haste every three months to see that he has the correct number of little punctures on his shoes.

He has a domestic roadster now, will have a French roadster if he lives long enough, and doubtless a Chinese tank if it comes into fashion. He looks like the advertisement of the young man rubbing his sunset-colored chest with liniment and goes East every other year to his class reunion.

I want you to meet his Love. Her name is Betty Medill, and she would take well in the movies. Her father gives her three hundred a month to dress on, and she has tawny eyes and hair and feather fans of five colors.

I shall also introduce her father, Cyrus Medill. Though he is to all appearances flesh and blood, he is, strange to say, commonly known in Toledo as the Aluminum Man. But when he sits in his club window with two or three Iron Men, and the White Pine Man, and the Brass Man, they look very much as you and I do, only more so, if you know what I mean.

During the Christmas holidays of 1919 there took place in Toledo, counting only the people with the italicized *the*, forty-one dinner parties, sixteen dances, six luncheons, male and female, twelve teas, four stag dinners, two weddings, and thirteen bridge parties. It was the cumulative effect of all this that moved Perry Parkhurst on the twenty-ninth day of December to a decision.

This Medill girl would marry him and she wouldn't marry him. She was having such a good time that she hated to take such a definite step. Meanwhile, their secret engagement had got so long that it seemed as if any day it might break off of its own weight.

A little man named Warburton, who knew it all, persuaded Perry to superman her, to get a marriage license and go up to the Medill house and tell her she'd have to marry him at once or call it off forever. So he presented himself, his heart, his license, and his ultimatum, and within five minutes they were in the midst of a violent quarrel, a burst of sporadic open fighting such as occurs near the end of all long wars and engagements.

It brought about one of those ghastly lapses in which two people who are in love pull up sharp, look at each other coolly and think it's all been a mistake. Afterward they usually kiss wholesomely and assure the other person it was all their fault. Say it all was my fault! Say it was! I want to hear you say it!

But while reconciliation was trembling in the air, while each was, in a measure, stalling it off, so that they might the more voluptuously and sentimentally enjoy it when it came, they were permanently interrupted by a twenty-minute phone call for Betty from a garrulous aunt.

At the end of eighteen minutes Perry Parkhurst, urged on by pride and suspicion and injured dignity, put on his long fur coat, picked up his light brown soft hat, and stalked out the door.

"It's all over," he muttered brokenly as he tried to jam his car into first. "It's all over— if I have to choke you for an hour, damn you!". The last to the car, which had been standing some time and was quite cold.

He drove downtown— that is, he got into a snow rut that led him downtown. He sat slouched down very low in his seat, much too dispirited to care where he went. In front of the Clarendon Hotel he was hailed from the sidewalk by a bad man named Baily, who had big teeth and lived at the hotel and had never been in love.

"Perry," said the bad man softly when the roadster drew up beside him at the curb, "I've got six quarts of the doggonedest still champagne you ever tasted. A third of it's yours, Perry, if you'll come upstairs and help Martin Macy and me drink it."

"Baily," said Perry tensely, "I'll drink your champagne. I'll drink every drop of it, I don't care if it kills me."

"Shut up, you nut!" said the bad man gently. "They don't put wood alcohol in champagne. This is the stuff that proves the world is more than six thousand years old. It's so ancient that the cork is petrified. You have to pull it with a stone drill."

"Take me upstairs," said Perry moodily. "If that cork sees my heart it'll fall out from pure mortification."

The room upstairs was full of those innocent hotel pictures of little girls eating apples and sitting in swings and talking to dogs. The other decorations were neckties and a pink man reading a pink paper devoted to ladies in pink tights.

"When you have to go into the highways and byways ——" said the pink man, looking reproachfully at Baily and Perry.

"Hello, Martin," said Perry shortly, "where's this stone-age champagne?"

"What's the rush? This isn't an operation, understand. This is a party."

Perry sat down dully and looked disapprovingly at all the neckties.

Baily leisurely opened the door of a wardrobe and brought out six handsome bottles.

"Take off that darn fur coat!" said Martin to Perry. "Or maybe you'd like to have us open all the windows."

"Give me champagne," said Perry.

"Going to the Townsends' circus ball tonight?"

"Am not!"

"'Invited?"

"Uh-huh."

"Why not go?"

"Oh, I'm sick of parties," exclaimed Perry. "I'm sick of them. I've been to so many that I'm sick of them."

"Maybe you're going to the Howard Tates' party?"

"No, I tell you; I'm sick of them."

"Well," said Macy consolingly, "the Tates' is just for college kids anyways."

"I tell you——"

"I thought you'd be going to one of them anyways. I see by the papers you haven't missed one this Christmas."

"Hm," grunted Perry morosely.

He would never go to any more parties. Classical phrases played in his mind— that side of his life was closed, closed. Now when a man says "closed, closed" like that, you can be pretty sure that some woman has double-closed him, so to speak.

Perry was also thinking that other classical thought, about how cowardly suicide is. A noble thought that one — warm and inspiring. Think of all the fine men we should lose if suicide were not so cowardly!

An hour later was six o'clock, and Perry had lost all resemblance to the young man in the liniment advertisement. He looked like a rough draft for a riotous cartoon. They were singing— an impromptu song of Baily's improvisation:

"One Lump Perry, the parlor snake,
Famous through the city for the way he drinks his tea;
Plays with it, toys with it
Makes no noise with it,
Balanced on a napkin on his well-trained knee—"

"Trouble is," said Perry, who had just banged his hair with Baily's comb and was tying an orange tie round it to get the effect of Julius Caesar, "that you fellas can't sing worth a damn. As soon as I leave the air and start singing tenor you start singing tenor too."

"I'm a natural tenor," said Macy gravely. "Voice lacks cultivation, that's all. Gotta natural voice, my aunt used to say. Naturally good singer."

"Singers, singers, all good singers," remarked Baily, who was at the telephone. "No, not the cabaret; I want night egg. I mean some dog-gone clerk that's got food— food! I want——"

"Julius Caesar," announced Perry, turning round from the mirror. "Man of iron will and stern determination."

"Shut up!" yelled Baily. "Say, this is Mr. Baily. Send up enormous supper. Use your own judgment. Right away."

He connected the receiver and the hook with some difficulty, and then with his lips closed and an expression of solemn intensity in his eyes went to the lower drawer of his dresser and pulled it open.

"Lookit!" he commanded. In his hands he held a truncated garment of pink gingham. "Pants," he exclaimed gravely. "Lookit!"

This was a pink blouse, a red tie, and a Buster Brown collar.

"Lookit!" he repeated. "Costume for the Townsends' circus ball. I'm little boy carries water for the elephants."

Perry was impressed in spite of himself.

"I'm going to be Julius Caesar," he announced after a moment of concentration.

"Thought you weren't going!" said Macy.

"Me? Sure I'm going, Never miss a party. Good for the nerves— like celery."

"Caesar!" scoffed Baily. "Can't be Caesar! He is not about a circus. Caesar's Shakespeare. Go as a clown."

Perry shook his head. "Nope; Caesar,"

"Caesar?"

"Sure. Chariot."

Light dawned on Baily. "That's right. Good idea."

Perry looked round the room searchingly. "You lend me a bathrobe and this tie," he said finally.

Baily considered. "No good."

"Sure, that's all I need. Caesar was a savage. They can't kick if I come as Caesar, if he was a savage."

"No," said Baily, shaking his head slowly. "Get a costume over at a costumer's. Over at Nolak's."

"Closed up."

"Find out."

After a puzzling five minutes at the phone a small, weary voice managed to convince Perry that it was Mr. Nolak speaking, and that they would remain open until eight because of the Townsends' ball. Thus assured, Perry ate a great amount of filet mignon and drank his third of the last bottle of champagne.

At eight-fifteen the man in the tall hat who stands in front of the Clarendon found him trying to start his roadster.

"Froze up," said Perry wisely. "The cold froze it. The cold air."

"Froze, eh?"

"Yes. Cold air froze it."

"Can't start it?"

"Nope. Let it stand here till summer. One of those hot old August days will thaw it out aright."

"Going to let it stand?"

"Sure. Let her stand. Take a hot thief to steal it. Get me a taxi."

The man in the tall hat summoned a taxi.

"Where to, mister?"

"Go to Nolak's— costume fella."

Chapter 2

Mrs. Nolak was short and ineffectual looking, and on the cessation of the world war had belonged for a while to one of the new nationalities. Owing to unsettled European conditions she had never since been quite sure what she was.

The shop in which she and her husband performed their daily stint was dim and ghostly, and peopled with suits of armor and Chinese mandarins, and enormous papier-mâché birds suspended from the ceiling.

In a vague background many rows of masks glared eyelessly at the visitor, and there were glass cases full of crowns and scepters, and jewels and enormous stomachers, and paints, and crape hair, and wigs of all colors.

When Perry ambled into the shop Mrs. Nolak was folding up the last troubles of a strenuous day, so she thought, in a drawer full of pink silk stockings.

"Something for you?" she queried pessimistically. "Want costume of Julius Hur, the charioteer."

Mrs. Nolak was sorry, but every stitch of charioteer had

been rented long ago. Was it for the Townsends' circus ball?

It was.

"Sorry," she said, "but I don't think there's anything left that's really circus."

This was an obstacle. "Hm," said Perry. An idea struck him suddenly. "If you've got a piece of canvas I could go as a tent."

"Sorry, but we haven't anything like that. A hardware store is where you'd have to go to. We have some very nice Confederate soldiers."

"No. No soldiers."

"And I have a very handsome king."

He shook his head.

"Several of the gentlemen" she continued hopefully, "are wearing stovepipe hats and swallow-tail coats and going as ringmasters— but we're all out of tall hats. I can let you have some crape hair for a mustache."

"Want something distinctive."

"Something— let's see. Well, we have a lion's head, and a goose, and a camel—"

"Camel?" The idea seized Perry's imagination, gripped it fiercely.

"Yes, but It needs two people."

"Camel, That's the idea. Let me see it."

The camel was produced from his resting place on a top shelf. At first glance he appeared to consist entirely of a very gaunt, cadaverous head and a sizable hump, but on being spread out he was found to possess a dark brown, unwholesome-looking body made of thick, cottony cloth.

"You see it takes two people," explained Mrs. Nolak, holding the camel in frank admiration. "If you have a friend he could be part of it. You see there's sorta pants for two people. One pair is for the fella in front, and the other pair for the fella in back. The fella in front does the looking out through these here eyes, and the fella in back he's just gotta stoop over and follow the front fella round."

"Put it on," commanded Perry.

Obediently Mrs. Nolak put her tabby-cat face inside the camel's head and turned it from side to side ferociously.

Perry was fascinated.

"What noise does a camel make?"

"What?" asked Mrs. Nolak as her face emerged, somewhat smudgy. "Oh, what noise? Why, he sorta brays."

"Let me see it in a mirror."

Before a wide mirror Perry tried on the head and turned from side to side appraisingly. In the dim light the effect was distinctly pleasing.

The camel's face was a study in pessimism, decorated with numerous abrasions, and it must be admitted that his coat was in that state of general negligence peculiar to camels— in fact, he needed to be cleaned and pressed— but distinctive he certainly was. He was majestic. He would have attracted attention in any gathering, if only by his melancholy cast of feature and the look of hunger lurking round his shadowy eyes.

"You see you have to have two people," said Mrs. Nolak again.

Perry tentatively gathered up the body and legs and

wrapped them about him, tying the hind legs as a girdle round his waist. The effect on the whole was bad. It was even irreverent— like one of those medieval pictures of a monk changed into a beast by the ministrations of Satan. At the very best the ensemble resembled a humpbacked cow sitting on her haunches among blankets.

"Don't look like anything at all," objected Perry gloomily.

"No," said Mrs. Nolak; "you see you got to have two people."

A solution flashed upon Perry.

"You got a date tonight?"

"Oh, I couldn't possibly——"

"Oh, come on," said Perry encouragingly. "Sure you can! Here! Be good sport, and climb into these hind legs."

With difficulty he located them, and extended their yawning depths ingratiatingly. But Mrs. Nolak seemed loath. She backed perversely away.

"Oh, no——"

"Come on! You can be the front if you want to. Or we'll flip a coin. Will make it worth your while."

Mrs. Nolak set her lips firmly together. "Now you just stop!" she said with no coyness implied. "None of the gentlemen ever acted up this way before. My husband ——"

"You got a husband?" demanded Perry. "Where is he?"

"He's home."

"What is the telephone number?"

After considerable parley he obtained the telephone

number pertaining to the Nolak penates and got into communication with that small, weary voice he had heard once before that day. But Mr. Nolak, though taken off his guard and somewhat confused by Perry's brilliant flow of logic, stuck staunchly to his point. He refused firmly, but with dignity, to help out Mr. Parkhurst in the capacity of back part of a camel.

Having rung off, or rather having been rung off on, Perry sat down on a three-legged stool to think it over. He named over to himself those friends on whom he might call, and then his mind paused as Betty Medill's name hazily and sorrowfully occurred to him. He had a sentimental thought. He would ask her. Their love affair was over, but she could not refuse this last request.

Surely it was not much to ask— to help him keep up his end of social obligation for one short night. And if she insisted, she could be the front part of the camel and he would go as the back. His magnanimity pleased him. His mind even turned to rosy-colored dreams of a tender reconciliation inside the camel— there hidden away from all the world....

"Now you'd better decide right off."

The bourgeois voice of Mrs. Nolak broke in upon his mellow fancies and roused him to action. He went to the phone and called up the Medill house. Miss Betty was out; had gone out to dinner.

Then, when all seemed lost, the camel's back wandered curiously into the store. He was a dilapidated individual with a cold in his head and a general trend about him of downwardness.

His cap was pulled down low on his head, and his chin

was pulled down low on his chest, his coat hung down to his shoes, he looked run-down, down at the heels, and— Salvation Army to the contrary— down and out.

He said that he was the taxicab-driver that the gentleman had hired at the Clarendon Hotel. He had been instructed to wait outside, but he had waited some time, and a suspicion had grown upon him that the gentleman had gone out the back way with purpose to defraud him— gentlemen sometimes did— so he had come in. He sank down onto the three-legged stool.

"Want to go to a party?" demanded Perry sternly.

"I gotta work," answered the taxi-driver lugubriously. "I gotta keep my job."

"It's a very good party."

"It's a very good job."

"Come on!" urged Perry. "Be a good fella. See— it's pretty!" He held the camel up and the taxi-driver looked at it cynically.

"Huh!"

Perry searched feverishly among the folds of the cloth.

"See!" he cried enthusiastically, holding up a selection of folds. "This is your part. You don't even have to talk. All you have to do is to walk— and sit down occasionally. You do all the sitting down. Think of it. I'm on my feet all the time and you can sit down some of the time. The only time I can sit down is when we're lying down, and you can sit down when— oh, any time. See?"

"What's that thing?" demanded the individual dubiously. "A shroud?"

"Not at all," said Perry indignantly. "It's a camel."

"Huh?"

Then Perry mentioned a sum of money, and the conversation left the land of grunts and assumed a practical tinge. Perry and the taxi-driver tried on the camel in front of the mirror.

"You can't see it," explained Perry, peering anxiously out through the eye holes, "but honestly, old man, you look simply great! Honestly!"

A grunt from the hump acknowledged this somewhat dubious compliment.

"Honestly, you look great!" repeated Perry enthusiastically. "Move round a little."

The hind legs moved forward, giving the effect of a huge cat-camel hunching his back preparatory to a spring.

"No; move sideways."

The camel's hips went neatly out of joint; a hula dancer would have writhed in envy.

"Good, isn't it?" demanded Perry, turning to Mrs. Nolak for approval.

"It looks lovely," agreed Mrs. Nolak.

"We'll take it," said Perry.

The bundle was stowed under Perry's arm and they left the shop.

"Go to the party!" he commanded as he took his seat in the back.

"What party?"

"Fancy-dress party."

"Where about is it?"

This presented a new problem. Perry tried to

remember, but the names of all those who had given parties during the holidays danced confusedly before his eyes. He could ask Mrs. Nolak, but on looking out the window he saw that the shop was dark. Mrs. Nolak had already faded out, a little black smudge far down the snowy street.

"Drive uptown," directed Perry with fine confidence. "If you see a party, stop. Otherwise I'll tell you when we get there."

He fell into a hazy daydream and his thoughts wandered again to Betty— he imagined vaguely that they had a disagreement because she refused to go to the party as the back part of the camel. He was just slipping off into a chilly doze when he was wakened by the taxi-driver opening the door and shaking him by the arm.

"Here we are, maybe."

Perry looked out sleepily. A striped awning led from the curb up to a spreading gray stone house, from which issued the low drummy whine of expensive jazz. He recognized the Howard Tate house.

"Sure," he said emphatically; "That's it! Tate's party tonight. Sure, everybody's going."

"Say," said the individual anxiously after another look at the awning, "you sure these people ain't gonna romp on me for coming here?"

Perry drew himself up with dignity.

"'If anybody says anything to you, just tell them you're part of my costume."

The visualization of himself as a thing rather than a person seemed to reassure the individual.

"All right," he said reluctantly.

Perry stepped out under the shelter of the awning and began unrolling the camel.

"Let's go," he commanded.

Several minutes later a melancholy, hungry-looking camel, emitting clouds of smoke from his mouth and from the tip of his noble hump, might have been seen crossing the threshold of the Howard Tate residence, passing a startled footman without so much as a snort, and heading directly for the main stairs that led up to the ballroom.

The beast walked with a peculiar gait which varied between an uncertain lockstep and a stampede— but can best be described by the word "halting." The camel had a halting gait— and as he walked he alternately elongated and contracted like a gigantic concertina.

Chapter 3

The Howard Tates are, as every one who lives in Toledo knows, the most formidable people in town. Mrs. Howard Tate was a Chicago Todd before she became a Toledo Tate, and the family generally affect that conscious simplicity which has begun to be the earmark of American aristocracy.

The Tates have reached the stage where they talk about pigs and farms and look at you icy-eyed if you are not amused. They have begun to prefer retainers rather than friends as dinner guests, spend a lot of money in a quiet way, and, having lost all sense of competition, are in the process of growing quite dull.

The dance this evening was for little Millicent Tate, and though all ages were represented, the dancers were mostly from school and college— the younger married crowd was at the Townsends' circus ball up at the Tallyho Club.

Mrs. Tate was standing just inside the ballroom, following Millicent round with her eyes, and beaming whenever she caught her bye. Beside her were two middle-aged sycophants, who were saying what a perfectly exquisite child Millicent was. It was at this moment that

Mrs. Tate was grasped firmly by the skirt and her youngest daughter, Emily, aged eleven, hurled herself with an "Oof!" into her mother's arms.

"Why, Emily, what's the trouble?"

"Mamma," said Emily, wild-eyed but voluble, "there's something out on the stairs."

"What?"

"There's a thing out on the stairs, mamma. I think it's a big dog, mamma, but it doesn't look like a dog."

"What do you mean, Emily?"

The sycophants waved their heads sympathetically.

"Mamma, it looks like a— like a camel."

Mrs. Tate laughed.

"You saw a mean old shadow, dear, that's all."

"No, I didn't. No, it was some kind of thing, mamma— big. I was going downstairs to see if there were any more people, and this dog or something, he was coming upstairs. Kinda funny, mamma, like he was lame. And then he saw me and gave a sort of growl, and then he slipped at the top of the landing, and I ran."

Mrs. Tate's laugh faded.

"The child must have seen something," she said.

The sycophants agreed that the child must have seen something— and suddenly all three women took an instinctive step away from the door as the sounds of muffled steps were audible just outside. And then three startled gasps rang out as a dark brown form rounded the corner, and they saw what was apparently a huge beast looking down at them hungrily.

"Oof!" cried Mrs. Tate.

"O-o-oh!" cried the ladies in a chorus.

The camel suddenly humped his back, and the gasps turned to shrieks.

"Oh— look!"

"What is it?"

The dancing stopped, but the dancers hurrying over got quite a different impression of the invader; in fact, the young people immediately suspected that it was a stunt, a hired entertainer come to amuse the party. The boys in long trousers looked at it rather disdainfully, and sauntered over with their hands in their pockets, feeling that their intelligence was being insulted. But the girls uttered little shouts of glee.

"It's a camel!"

"Well, if he isn't the funniest!"

The camel stood there uncertainly, swaying slightly from side to aide, and seeming to take in the room in a careful, appraising glance; then as if he had come to an abrupt decision, he turned and ambled swiftly out the door.

Mr. Howard Tate had just come out of the library on the lower floor, and was standing chatting with a young man in the hall. Suddenly they heard the noise of shouting upstairs, and almost immediately a succession of bumping sounds, followed by the precipitous appearance at the foot of the stairway of a large brown beast that seemed to be going somewhere in a great hurry.

"Now what the devil!" said Mr. Tate, starting.

The beast picked itself up not without dignity and,

affecting an air of extreme nonchalance, as if he had just remembered an important engagement, started at a mixed gait toward the front door. In fact, his front legs began casually to run.

"See here now," said Mr. Tate sternly. "Here! Grab it, Butterfield! Grab it!"

The young man enveloped the rear of the camel in a pair of compelling arms, and, realizing that further locomotion was impossible, the front end submitted to capture and stood resignedly in a state of some agitation. By this time a flood of young people was pouring downstairs, and Mr. Tate, suspecting everything from an ingenious burglar to an escaped lunatic, gave crisp directions to the young man:

"Hold him! Lead him in here; we'll soon see."

The camel consented to be led into the library, and Mr. Tate, after locking the door, took a revolver from a table drawer and instructed the young man to take the thing's head off. Then he gasped and returned the revolver to its hiding-place. "Well, Perry Parkhurst!" he exclaimed in amazement.

"Got the wrong party, Mr. Tate," said Perry sheepishly. "Hope I didn't scare you."

"Well— you gave us a thrill, Perry." Realization dawned on him. "You're bound for the Townsends' circus ball."

"That's the general idea."

"Let me introduce Mr. Butterfield, Mr. Parkhurst." Then turning to Perry; "Butterfield is staying with us for a few days."

"I got a little mixed up," mumbled Perry. "I'm very sorry."

"Perfectly all right; most natural mistake in the world. I've got a clown rig and I'm going down there myself after a while." He turned to Butterfield. "Better change your mind and come down with us."

The young man demurred. He was going to bed.

"Have a drink, Perry?" suggested Mr. Tate.

"Thanks, I will."

"And, say," continued Tate quickly, "I'd forgotten all about your— friend here." He indicated the rear part of the camel. "I didn't mean to seem discourteous. Is it any one I know? Bring him out."

"It's not a friend," explained Perry hurriedly. "I just rented him."

"Does he drink?"

"Do you?" demanded Perry, twisting himself tortuously round.

There was a faint sound of assent.

"Sure he does!" said Mr. Tate heartily. "A really efficient camel ought to be able to drink enough so it'd last him three days."

"Tell you," said Perry anxiously, "he isn't exactly dressed up enough to come out. If you give me the bottle I can hand it back to him and he can take his inside."

From under the cloth was audible the enthusiastic smacking sound inspired by this suggestion. When a butler had appeared with bottles, glasses, and siphon one of the bottles was handed back; thereafter the silent partner could be heard imbibing long potations at frequent intervals.

Thus passed a benign hour. At ten o'clock Mr. Tate decided that they'd better be starting. He donned his clown's costume; Perry replaced the camel's head, arid side by side they traversed on foot the single block between the Tate house and the Tallyho Club.

The circus ball was in full swing. A great tent fly had been put up inside the ballroom and round the walls had been built rows of booths representing the various attractions of a circus side show, but these were now vacated and over the floor swarmed a shouting, laughing medley of youth and color— clowns, bearded ladies, acrobats, bareback riders, ringmasters, tattooed men, and charioteers.

The Townsends had determined to assure their party of success, so a great quantity of liquor had been surreptitiously brought over from their house and was now flowing freely. A green ribbon ran along the wall completely round the ballroom, with pointing arrows alongside and signs which instructed the uninitiated to "Follow the green line!" The green line led down to the bar, where waited pure punch and wicked punch and plain dark-green bottles.

On the wall above the bar was another arrow, red and very wavy, and under it the slogan: "Now follow this!"

But even amid the luxury of costume and high spirits represented, there, the entrance of the camel created something of a stir, and Perry was immediately surrounded by a curious, laughing crowd attempting to penetrate the identity of this beast that stood by the wide doorway eyeing the dancers with his hungry, melancholy gaze.

And then Perry saw Betty standing in front of a booth, talking to a comic policeman. She was dressed in the costume of an Egyptian snake-charmer: her tawny hair was braided and drawn through brass rings, the effect crowned with a glittering Oriental tiara. Her fair face was stained to a warm olive glow and on her arms and the half moon of her back writhed painted serpents with single eyes of venomous green.

Her feet were in sandals and her skirt was slit to the knees, so that when she walked one caught a glimpse of other slim serpents painted just above her bare ankles. Wound about her neck was a glittering cobra. Altogether a charming costume— one that caused the more nervous among the older women to shrink away from her when she passed, and the more troublesome ones to make great talk about "shouldn't be allowed" and "perfectly disgraceful."

But Perry, peering through the uncertain eyes of the camel, saw only her face, radiant, animated, and glowing with excitement, and her arms and shoulders, whose mobile, expressive gestures made her always the outstanding figure in any group.

He was fascinated and his fascination exercised a sobering effect on him. With a growing clarity the events of the day came back— rage rose within him, and with a half-formed intention of taking her away from the crowd he started toward her— or rather he elongated slightly, for he had neglected to issue the preparatory command necessary to locomotion.

But at this point fickle Kismet, who for a day had played with him bitterly and sardonically, decided to reward him in full for the amusement he had afforded her. Kismet turned the tawny eyes of the snake-charmer to the camel. Kismet led her to lean toward the man beside her and say, "Who's that? That camel?"

"Darned if I know."

But a little man named Warburton, who knew it all, found it necessary to hazard an opinion: "It came in with Mr. Tate. I think part of it's probably Warren Butterfield, the architect from New York, who's visiting the Tates."

Something stirred in Betty Medill— that age-old interest of the provincial girl in the visiting man. "Oh," she said casually after a slight pause.

At the end of the next dance Betty and her partner finished up within a few feet of the camel. With the informal audacity that was the keynote of the evening she reached out and gently rubbed the camel's nose.

"Hello, old camel." The camel stirred uneasily.

"You afraid of me?" said Betty, lifting her eyebrows in reproof. "Don't be. You see I'm a snake-charmer, but I'm pretty good at camels too."

The camel bowed very low and someone made the obvious remark about beauty and the beast.

Mrs. Townsend approached the group.

"Well, Mr. Butterfield," she said helpfully, "I wouldn't have recognized you."

Perry bowed again and smiled gleefully behind his mask.

"And who is this with you?" she inquired.

"Oh," said Perry, his voice muffled by the thick cloth and quite unrecognizable, "he isn't a fellow, Mrs. Townsend. He's just part of my costume."

Mrs. Townsend laughed and moved away. Perry turned again to Betty,

"So," he thought, "this is how much she cares! On the

very day of our final rupture she starts a flirtation with another man— an absolute stranger."

On an impulse he gave her a soft nudge with his shoulder and waved his head suggestively toward the hall, making it clear that he desired her to leave her partner and accompany him.

"By-by, Rus," she called to her partner. "This old camel's got me. Where we going, Prince of Beasts?"

The noble animal made no rejoinder, but stalked gravely along in the direction of a secluded nook on the side stairs. There she seated herself, and the camel, after some seconds of confusion which included gruff orders and sounds of a heated dispute going on in his interior, placed himself beside her— his hind legs stretching out uncomfortably across two steps.

"Well, old egg," said Betty cheerfully, "how do you like our happy party?"

The old egg indicated that he liked it by rolling his head ecstatically and executing a gleeful kick with his hoofs.

"This is the first time that I ever had a tête-à-tête with a man's valet around"— she pointed to the hind legs— "or whatever that is."

"Oh," mumbled Perry, "he's deaf and blind."

"I should think you'd feel rather handicapped— you can't very well toddle, even if you want to."

The camel hang his head lugubriously.

"I wish you'd say something," continued Betty sweetly. "Say you like me, camel. Say you think I'm beautiful. Say you'd like to belong to a pretty snake-charmer."

The camel would.

"Will you dance with me, camel?"

The camel would try.

Betty devoted half an hour to the camel. She devoted at least half an hour to all visiting men. It was usually sufficient. When she approached a new man the current débutantes were accustomed to scatter right and left like a close column deploying before a machine-gun. And so to Perry Parkhurst was awarded the unique privilege of seeing his love as others saw her. He was flirted with violently!

Chapter 4

This paradise of frail foundation was broken into by the sounds of a general ingress to the ballroom; the cotillion was beginning. Betty and the camel joined the crowd, her brown hand resting lightly on his shoulder, defiantly symbolizing her complete adoption of him.

When they entered the couples were already seating themselves at tables round the walls, and Mrs. Townsend, resplendent as a super bareback rider with rather too rotund calves, was standing in the center with the ringmaster in charge of arrangements. At a signal to the band every one rose and began to dance.

"Isn't it just slick!" sighed Betty. "Do you think you can possibly dance?"

Perry nodded enthusiastically. He felt suddenly exuberant. After all, he was here incognito talking to his love— he could wink patronizingly at the world.

So Perry danced the cotillion. I say danced, but that is stretching the word far beyond the wildest dreams of the jazziest terpsichorean. He suffered his partner to put her hands on his helpless shoulders and pull him here and there over the floor while he hung his huge head docilely over her shoulder and made futile dummy motions with his feet.

His hind legs danced in a manner all their own, chiefly by hopping first on one foot and then on the other. Never being sure whether dancing was going on or not, the hind legs played safe by going through a series of steps whenever the music started playing. So the spectacle was frequently presented of the front part of the camel standing at ease and the rear keeping up a constant energetic motion calculated to rouse a sympathetic perspiration in any soft-hearted observer.

He was frequently favored. He danced first with a tall lady covered with straw who announced jovially that she was a bale of hay and coyly begged him not to eat her.

"I'd like to; you're so sweet," said the camel gallantly.

Each time the ringmaster shouted his call of "Men up!" he lumbered ferociously for Betty with the cardboard wienerwurst or the photograph of the bearded lady or whatever the favor chanced to be. Sometimes he reached her first, but usually his rushes were unsuccessful and resulted in intense interior arguments.

"For Heaven's sake," Perry would snarl, fiercely between his clenched teeth, "get a little pep! I could have gotten her that time if you'd picked your feet up."

"Well, gimme a little warning!"

"I did, darn you."

"I can't see a dog-gone thing in here."

"All you have to do is follow me. It's just like dragging a load of sand round to walk with you."

"Maybe you want to try back here."

"You shut up! If these people found you in this room they'd give you the worst beating you ever had. They'd take your taxi license away from you!"

Perry surprised himself by the ease with which he made this monstrous threat, but it seemed to have a soporific influence on his companion, for he gave out an "aw gwan" and subsided into abashed silence.

The ringmaster mounted to the top of the piano and waved his hand for silence.

"Prizes!" he cried. "Gather round!"

"Yea! Prizes!"

Self-consciously the circle swayed forward. The rather pretty girl who had mustered the nerve to come as a bearded lady trembled with excitement, thinking to be rewarded for an evening's hideousness. The man who had spent the afternoon having tattoo marks painted on him skulked on the edge of the crowd, blushing furiously when any one told him he was sure to get it.

"Lady and gent performers of this circus," announced the ringmaster jovially, "I am sure we will all agree that a good time has been had by all. We will now bestow honor where honor is due by bestowing the prizes. Mrs. Townsend has asked me to bestow the prices. Now, fellow performers, the first prize is for that lady who has displayed this evening the most striking, becoming"— at this point the bearded lady sighed resignedly— "and original costume." Here the bale of hay pricked up her ears.

"Now I am sure that the decision which has been agreed upon will be unanimous with all here present. The first prize goes to Miss Betty Medill, the charming Egyptian snake-charmer."

There was a burst of applause, chiefly masculine, and Miss Betty Medill, blushing beautifully through her olive paint, was passed up to receive her award. With a tender glance the ringmaster handed down to her a huge bouquet of orchids.

"And now," he continued, looking round him, "the other prize is for that man who has the most amusing and original costume. This prize goes without dispute to a guest in our midst, a gentleman who is visiting here but whose stay we all hope will be long and merry— in short, to the noble camel who has entertained us all by his hungry look and his brilliant dancing throughout the evening."

He ceased and there was a violent clapping, and yeaing, for it was a popular choice. The prize, a large box of cigars, was put aside for the camel, as he was anatomically unable to accept it in person.

"And now," continued the ringmaster, "we will wind up the cotillion with the marriage of Mirth to Folly!

"Form for the grand wedding march, the beautiful snake-charmer and the noble camel in front!"

Betty skipped forward cheerily and wound an olive arm round the camel's neck. Behind them formed the procession of little boys, little girls, country jakes, fat ladies, thin men, sword-swallowers, wild men of Borneo, and armless wonders, many of them well in their cups, all of them excited and happy and dazzled by the flow of light and color round them, and by the familiar faces, strangely unfamiliar under bizarre wigs and barbaric paint.

The voluptuous chords of the wedding march done in blasphemous syncopation issued in a delirious blend from the trombones and saxophones— and the march began.

"Aren't you glad, camel?" demanded Betty sweetly as they stepped off. "Aren't you glad we're going to be married and you're going to belong to the nice snake-charmer ever afterward?"

The camel's front legs pranced, expressing excessive joy.

"Minister! Minister! Where's the minister?" cried voices out of the revel. "Who's going to be the clergyman?"

The head of Jumbo, obese negro, waiter at the Tally-ho Club for many years, appeared rashly through a half-opened pantry door.

"Oh, Jumbo!"

"Get old Jumbo. He's the fella!"

"Come on, Jumbo. How 'bout marrying us a couple?"

"Yea!"

Jumbo was seized by four comedians, stripped of his apron, and escorted to a raised daïs at the head of the ball. There his collar was removed and replaced back side forward with ecclesiastical effect. The parade separated into two lines, leaving an aisle for the bride and groom.

"Lawdy, man," roared Jumbo, "Ah got old Bible and everything, sure enough."

He produced a battered Bible from an interior pocket.

"Yea! Jumbo's got a Bible!"

"Razor, too, I'll bet!"

Together the snake-charmer and the camel ascended

the cheering aisle and stopped in front of Jumbo.

"Where's your license, camel?"

A man near by prodded Perry.

"Give him a piece of paper. Anything will do."

Perry fumbled confusedly in his pocket, found a folded paper, and pushed it out through the camel's mouth. Holding it upside down Jumbo pretended to scan it earnestly.

"This yeah's a special camel's license," he said. "Get your ring ready, camel."

Inside the camel Perry turned round and addressed his worse half.

"Give me a ring, for Heaven's sake!"

"I ain't got none," protested a weary voice.

"You have. I saw it."

"I ain't going to take it off my hand."

"If you don't I'll kill you."

There was a gasp and Perry felt a huge affair of rhinestone and brass inserted into his hand.

Again he was nudged from the outside.

"Speak up!"

"I do!" cried Perry quickly.

He heard Betty's responses given in a debonair tone, and even in this burlesque the sound thrilled him. Then he had pushed the rhinestone through a tear in the camel's coat and was slipping it on her finger, muttering ancient and historic words after Jumbo. He didn't want anyone to know about this ever. His one idea was to slip away without having to disclose his identity, for Mr. Tate had so

far kept his secret well. A dignified young man, Perry—
and this might injure his infant law practice.

"Embrace the bride!"

"Unmask, camel, and kiss her!"

Instinctively his heart beat high as Betty turned to him
laughingly and began to strike the cardboard muzzle. He
felt his self-control giving way, he longed to surround her
with his arms and declare his identity and kiss those lips
that smiled only a foot away— when suddenly the laughter
and applause round them died off and a curious hush fell
over the hall.

Perry and Betty looked up in surprise. Jumbo had given
vent to a huge "Hello!" in such a startled voice that all eyes
were bent on him.

"Hello!" he said again. He had turned round the camel's
marriage license, which he had been holding upside down,
produced spectacles, and was studying it agonizingly.

"Why," he exclaimed, and in the pervading silence his
words were heard plainly by everyone in the room, "this
yeah's a sure enough marriage permit."

"What?"

"Huh?"

"Say it again, Jumbo!"

"Sure you can read?"

Jumbo waved them to silence and Perry's blood burned
to fire in his veins as he realized the break he had made.

"Yassuh!" repeated Jumbo. "This yeah's a sure enough
license, and the parties concerned one of them is this yeah
young lady, Miss Betty Medill, and the other's Mister Perry
Parkhurst."

There was a general gasp, and a low rumble broke out as all eyes fell on the camel. Betty shrank away from him quickly, her tawny eyes giving out sparks of fury.

"Are you Mister Parkhurst, you camel?"

Perry made no answer. The crowd pressed up closer and stared at him. He stood frozen rigid with embarrassment, his cardboard face still hungry and sardonic as he regarded the ominous Jumbo.

"You all better speak up!" said Jumbo slowly, "this yeah's a mighty serious matter. Outside my duties at this club I happen to be a sure enough minister in the First Colored Baptist Church. It does look to me as though y'all is gone and got married."

Chapter 5

The scene that followed will go down forever in the annals of the Tallyho Club. Stout matrons fainted, one hundred percent Americans swore, wild-eyed débutantes babbled in lightning groups instantly formed and instantly dissolved, and a great buzz of chatter, virulent yet oddly subdued, hummed through the chaotic ballroom.

Feverish youths swore they would kill Perry or Jumbo or themselves or someone, and the Baptist preacher was besieged by a tempestuous covey of clamorous amateur lawyers, asking questions, making threats, demanding precedents, ordering the bonds annulled, and especially trying to ferret out any hint of prearrangement in what had occurred.

In the corner Mrs. Townsend was crying softly on the shoulder of Mr. Howard Tate, who was trying vainly to comfort her; they were exchanging "all my fault's" volubly and voluminously.

Outside on a snow-covered walk Mr. Cyrus Medill, the Aluminum Man, was being paced slowly up and down between two brawny charioteers, giving vent now to a string of unrepeatables, now to wild pleadings that they'd just let him get at Jumbo. He was facetiously attired for the evening as a wild man of Borneo, and the most exacting stage-manager would have acknowledged any improvement in casting the part to be quite impossible.

Meanwhile the two principals held the real center of the stage. Betty Medill— or was it Betty Parkhurst?— storming furiously, was surrounded by the plainer girls— the prettier ones were too busy talking about her to pay much attention to her— and over on the other side of the hall stood the camel, still intact except for his headpiece, which dangled pathetically on his chest.

Perry was earnestly engaged in making protestations of his innocence to a ring of angry, puzzled men. Every few minutes, just as he had apparently proved his case, someone would mention the marriage certificate, and the inquisition would begin again.

A girl named Marion Cloud, considered the second best belle of Toledo, changed the gist of the situation by a remark she made to Betty.

"Well," she said maliciously, "it'll all blow over, dear. The courts will annul it without question."

Betty's angry tears dried miraculously in her eyes, her lips shut tight together, and she looked stonily at Marion. Then she rose and, scattering her sympathizers right and left, walked directly across the room to Perry, who stared at her in terror. Again silence crept down upon the room.

"Will you have the decency to grant me five minutes' conversation— or wasn't that included in your plans?"

He nodded, his mouth unable to form words. Indicating coldly that he was to follow her she walked out into the hall with her chin uptilted and headed for the privacy of one of the little card-rooms. Perry started after her, but was brought to a jerky halt by the failure of his hind legs to function.

"You stay here!" he commanded savagely.

"I can't," whined a voice from the hump, "unless you get out first and let me get out."

Perry hesitated, but unable any longer to tolerate the eyes of the curious crowd he muttered a command and the camel moved carefully from the room on its four legs. Betty was waiting for him.

"Well," she began furiously, "you see what you've done! You and that crazy license! I told you you shouldn't have gotten it!"

"My dear girl, I—"

"Don't say 'dear girl' to me! Save that for your real wife if you ever get one after this disgraceful performance. And don't try to pretend it wasn't all arranged. You know you gave that colored waiter money! You know you did! Do you mean to say you didn't try to marry me?"

"No— of course—"

"Yes, you'd better admit it! You tried it, and now what are you going to do? Do you know my father's nearly crazy? It'll serve you right if he tries to kill you. He'll take his gun and put some cold steel in you. Even if this wed— this thing can be annulled it'll hang over me all the rest of my life!"

Perry could not resist quoting softly: "'Oh, camel, wouldn't you like to belong to the pretty snake-charmer for all your—"

"Shut-up!" cried Betty.

There was a pause.

"Betty," said Perry finally, "there's only one thing to do that will really get us out clear. That's for you to marry me."

"Marry you!"

"Yes. Really it's the only—"

"You shut up! I wouldn't marry you if— if—"

"I know. If I were the last man on earth. But if you care anything about your reputation—"

"Reputation!" she cried. "You're a nice one to think about my reputation now. Why didn't you think about my reputation before you hired that horrible Jumbo to— to —"

Perry tossed up his hands hopelessly. "Very well. I'll do anything you want. Lord knows I renounce all claims!"

"But," said a new voice, "I don't."

Perry and Betty started, and she put her hand to her heart.

"For Heaven's sake, what was that?"

"It's me," said the camel's back.

In a minute Perry had whipped off the camel's skin, and a lax, limp object, his clothes hanging on him damply, his hand clenched tightly on an almost empty bottle, stood defiantly before them.

"Oh," cried Betty, "you brought that object in here to frighten me! You told me he was deaf— that awful person!"

The camel's back sat down on a chair with a sigh of satisfaction.

"Don't talk that way about me, lady. I ain't no person. I'm your husband."

"Husband!"

The cry was wrung simultaneously from Betty and Perry.

"Why, sure. I'm as much your husband as that gink is. The smoke didn't marry you to the camel's front. He married you to the whole camel. Why, that's my ring you got on your finger!"

With a little yelp she snatched the ring from her finger and flung it passionately at the floor.

"What's all this?" demanded Perry dazedly.

"Just that you better fix me and fix me right. If you don't I'm gonna have the same claim you got to being married to her!"

"That's bigamy," said Perry, turning gravely to Betty.

Then came the supreme moment of Perry's evening, the ultimate chance on which he risked his fortunes. He rose and looked first at Betty, where she sat weakly, aghast at this new complication, and then at the individual who swayed from side to side on his chair, uncertainly, menacingly.

"Very well," said Perry slowly to the individual, "you can have her. Betty, I'm going to prove to you that as far as I'm concerned our marriage was entirely accidental. I'm going to renounce utterly my rights to have you as my wife, and give you to— to the man whose ring you wear— your lawful husband."

There was a pause and four horror-stricken eyes were turned on him,

"Good-by, Betty," he said brokenly. "Don't forget me in your new-found happiness. I'm going to leave for the Far West on the morning train. Think of me kindly, Betty."

With a last glance at them he turned and his head rested on his chest as his hand touched the doorknob.

"Good-by," he repeated. He turned the doorknob.

But at this sound the snakes and silk and tawny hair precipitated themselves violently toward him.

"Oh, Perry, don't leave me! Perry, Perry, take me with you!"

Her tears flowed damply on his neck. Calmly he folded his arms about her.

"I don't care," she cried. "I love you and if you can wake up a minister at this hour and have it done over again I'll go West with you."

Over her shoulder the front part of the camel looked at the back part of the camel— and they exchanged a particularly subtle, esoteric sort of wink that only true camels can understand.

"It was an age of miracles, it was an age of art, it was an age of excess, and it was an age of satire."

Scott Fitzgerald

The Jazz Age

The Jazz Age, a name coined by Scott Fitzgerald, began in 1918 with the end of World War I and lasted until 1928, ending with the Stock Market Crash of October 1929.

The period, called the "Roaring Twenties", was marked by economic prosperity, cultural flowering, liberal behavior, social mobility, bootleg liquor, a shaking up of social mores, and most notably Jazz Music.

Jazz is the hybrid of African and European influences. From African influence, Jazz got its rhythm and blues quality and the tradition of playing or singing in one's own expressive way. From European influence, Jazz got its harmony and instruments. Both influences used improvisation which became a large part of Jazz.

What made Jazz so controversial was that it literally broke all the rules, including traditional musical theory.

However, Jazz was not the only art form of this period that reacted to changing times by changing its rules. Many writers began to deviate from the literary forms and rules that had defined the previous generation. The Jazz Age can be defined as a cultural movement, since it influenced every aspect of art and literature in the period.

Scott Fitzgerald ascribed the loosening of American sexual mores to teenagers' acquisition of automobiles during the First World War. However, one major motivating factor contributing to the genesis of the Jazz Age was the prohibition of alcohol.

Prohibition drove America's drinking population into speakeasies, underground night clubs where people could enjoy their booze and the newly popular Jazz music. Because these clubs were "underground," they were also open to new forms of expression and Jazz music was popularized in these bars.

The Nineteenth Amendment granted women the right to vote, and the speakeasies were the first place in America where it became acceptable for a woman who wasn't a prostitute to drink and smoke in public.

With women now taking part in the workforce after the end of the First World War there were many more possibilities for women in terms of social life and entertainment.

Ideas such as equality and free sexuality were very popular during the time and women seemed to capitalize during this period. Sexual mores loosened and youth-centric culture flourished.

Young people used the influence of jazz to rebel against the traditional culture of previous generations.

A new generation of young women, flappers, wore short skirts, bobbed their hair, listened to jazz, and flaunted their disdain for what was then considered acceptable behavior.

Flappers were seen as brash for wearing excessive makeup, drinking, treating sex in a casual manner, smoking, driving automobiles, and otherwise flouting social and sexual norms.

Psychoanalysis became fashionable among the wealthy, who happily shed their inhibitions with Sigmund Freud's approval. Erica Jong's "Fear of Flying" would have been a welcome addition to the period's literature, if it was not released forty years later in the early seventies.

"I have written a story. It is not about the younger generation. The hero is twenty-nine."

Scott Fitzgerald

Scott Fitzgerald

Francis Scott Key Fitzgerald, was born on September 24, 1896. In 1920 Fitzgerald succeeded in publishing his first novel, "This Side of Paradise." Earlier drafts of the same book were rejected twice before. After each rejection Scott rewrote and edited the book and finally, at the age of 21 he was published, a major achievement.

Just days after "This Side of Paradise" was published, Fitzgerald married a flapper, Zelda Sayre. If Fitzgerald had been trying to find a woman who could have been a character in one of his books, he succeeded in Zelda. She went on to suffer several famous nervous breakdowns which became the subject of Fitzgerald's fourth novel, "Tender is the Night."

In 1925 Fitzgerald published what many consider to be his masterpiece, "The Great Gatsby." The novel expertly portrayed social issues that characterized the time including; new versus old wealth, social class, and changing morals.

Fitzgerald wrote the 'The Great Gatsby' in Europe, while in Paris, the Riviera, and Italy. The twilight mood of the novel might have been suggested by its author's European stay as the Continent was slowly emerging from the horrors of the First World War.

When "The Great Gatsby" was published, Scott Fitzgerald, living high in France after his early success, cabled Max Perkins, his editor at Scribners, and asked if the news was good. It was not, the book received some reviews that were dismissive. For a writer of Fitzgerald's fame, sales were mediocre— about twenty thousand copies by the end of the year.

Scribners did a second printing, of three thousand copies, but that was it, and when Fitzgerald died, in 1940, half-forgotten at the age of forty-four, the book was hard to find.

His last royalty check, received August 1940, was for a double-unlucky $13.13; four months later he died of heart failure at the age of 44. For the entire year, only about 15 copies of The Great Gatsby had sold.

Within a decade, however, a "revival" of Fitzgerald's work began to influence both scholars and readers, and in 2013 his publisher, Scribner's, estimated that some 25 million copies of Gatsby have been sold worldwide— a far cry from the fewer than 25,000 moved during his lifetime.

Scott was an alcoholic, and no doubt his health would have declined, whatever the commercial fate of his masterpiece. But he was a writer who needed recognition and money as much as booze, and if "Gatsby" had sold well it would likely have saved him from the lacerating public confessions of failure that he made in the thirties. The book currently sells half a million copies a year.

While he achieved limited success in his lifetime, Scott Fitzgerald is now widely regarded as one of the greatest American writers of the 20th century. He is variously remembered as the "Great American Dreamer," the author of "The Great Gatsby", and the man who coined the phrase the "Jazz Age."

www.ingramcontent.com/pod-product-compliance
Lightning Source LLC
Chambersburg PA
CBHW020810130626
46554CB00006B/2370